THE LANGUAGE OF
chocolates

The Language of Chocolates
Copyright © Bruno D'Arcy 2008

All rights reserved. No part of this book may be reproduced
or transmitted in any form without the prior permission
of the author, except in the case
of brief quotations for use in reviews etc.

ISBN 978-1-4092-0248-6

Published by
Chocolate Boat Press/Lulu.com
chocolateboat@googlemail.com

Cover photo copyright © iStockphoto.com/Jill Chen
Cover by Pillow Design/Bruno Ferrari

For Sue

'It was – really, it was absolutely – oh, the most – it was simply – in fact, from that moment Edna knew that life could never be the same. She drew her hand away from Jimmy's, leaned back, and shut the chocolate box for ever. This at last was Love!'

(A demonstration of the transforming power of chocolates from Katherine Mansfield's Taking the Veil.)

PREFACE

Chocolates, particularly the more expensive, self-selected variety are both the jewels of confectionery and a way of seeing things: a pleasing perception, a certain happiness, a love or an affection, as seen through poetical spectacles. The insights, images and definitions that follow are chocolates too – frames of mind with some sweetness in them. Delicious rather than precious, they are born of a real fondness for the art and belie any hint of indulgent excess. *The Language of Chocolates* is a above all a book for ruminants to graze through. Wherever it is read, among friends, loved-ones or alone, a pleasing glow lingers long after it is finished. Treat it as you would a favoured box of truffles, ganaches and pralines: sample as many or as few of the entries as suits your mood, or follow the assortment in sequence for as long as the appetite allows. And if today the book consists mainly of witticisms, it is because tomorrow it will be choc-full of verities.

1

The path to heaven is paved with chocolates.

2

There is only one thing better than a chocolate and that is another chocolate.

3

Into your life let truffles fall, as Madame de Pompadour said truffles should fall, like a constant, bountiful yes.

4

The days are there to be enjoyed: the week ahead beckons like seven significant chocolates.

5

Genealogically, every chocolate is another relation of elation.

6

Sometimes one feels, subtly, that one is a ganache all day long.

7

In the exquisite moment of a chocolate time is put in parentheses.

8

What a difference a chocolate makes!

9

The shiny surface of a praline is where the two worlds meet – the world of the real and the world of the artificial. But which is which? At least one can eat a praline.

10

CHOCOPHORIA: The elation which follows the eating of chocolates. A feeling echoed by the Swiss mercenary in Bernard Shaw's *Arms and the Man* when he exclaims, 'To my last hour I shall remember those three chocolate creams'; and as described by Jean-Paul Aron, French philosopher and founder-member of the prestigious *Club des Croqueurs de Chocolat*: 'An intense aesthetic pleasure, unparalleled, sensuous, almost erotic'.

11

Bite by bite, nibble by nibble, chocolates are magnified by satisfaction till the last morsel is an apex of pleasure, from which we look down on the world and sigh.

12

Life should be one long succession of chocolates occasionally punctuated with chocolates.

13

A chocolate does not necessarily have to be eaten to be appreciated. It could be intimated, for example, in the shade of a lacy bodice, shaded by a feathered hat, shaded by a chestnut tree susurrating in France.

14

Hope that one day this ecstasy comes over you – you see the world from afar and it is a truffle.

15

'Let us roll all our strength and all our sweetness up into a ball.'

– Andrew Marvell's 17th century recipe for chocolate truffles?

16

A sweet missive in a moiré envelope, a chocolate is often a *billet doux* to the heart.

17

Liselette, Andalousie, Sylvia, Salvador, Rigoletto, Valencia: how silky sweet sound the names of our favourite chocolates, like softest music to attentive ears.

18

Know, too, that moussey ganache fillings echo in the folds, in the pleats, and in the ruches of festoons.

19

Is it convention or conviction that determines the names of chocolates are invariably synonyms of bliss?

20

CHOCOLATIST: Someone dedicated to seeking out and writing down the names of chocolates – names such as Liberty, Cascade, Romain and Fabiola – for the evocative allusions they inspire.

21

CHOCOPHONE: A word like nectar, climax or serene, which sounds as if it should be the name of a chocolate.

22

Sometimes a beautifully crafted ganache is desired, at other times just the thought of a paper-thin couverture breaking gently, aromatically, on the teeth is enough . . .

23

'Rhapsody' is one of those words which sound as if it should be full of crunchy hazelnut praline.

24

Footsteps leading to, but not away from, the dark moussey truffles. An immaculate consumption.

25

Gracious profusion of spring blossom, lush abandon of summer fruits, unutterable lilac-tinted sunsets – such florid images can only hint at what ganaches mean.

26

Some chocolates are so real everything else is but a dream.

27

There are so many joys in the world, will there ever be enough truffles to contain them?

28

EIDETIC MEMORY: The mental faculty of being able to reproduce, with vivid precision, the image of something seen recently or in the distant past. A useful ability in the game of chess, it is essential in the pursuit of chocolates.

29

My name is Panache. All over the world chocolates are falling in love with me.

30

If chocolates were to suddenly disappear from life, I wonder which part of your body would miss them the most?

31

CHOCOLAPSE: An absence of chocolates. Was *Bleak House* so-called because there were no chocolates? Dickens intimates as much when Richard and Ada visit the old Chancery in London, and the hostess greets them with the apology, 'I am sorry, but I cannot offer chocolate'.

32

As Alexander Pope almost put it: a little chocolate is a dangerous thing, not enough is positively fatal.

33

There is no perturbation greater than an absence of chocolates.

34

It is said that nature abhors a vacuum. It follows, therefore, that the quickest way to obtain chocolates is not to have any in the first place.

35

NATURAL SELECTION: The mechanism by which the best chocolates are invariably chosen first.

36

We do not choose our chocolates. Our chocolates choose us.

37

'Pretty, decorative, fanciful, where every contour is a celebration, chocolates are wholly Rococo in their disposition.'

— A note found in Madame de Pompadour's escritoire.

38

'The gap between one chocolate and another is no bigger than the eye of a needle; only a saint can pass through it.'

— Elizabeth Vigée-Lebrun, the beautiful and articulate painter at the court of Marie-Antoinette.

39

Her words would hang in the air like chocolates on a Christmas tree.

40

And when the milk chocolates melted her heart would freeze.

41

'It is those lively decorative outlines modulated by smooth rhythmic surfaces that create such appealing combinations of refinement and spontaneity in chocolates.'

— From a letter written by Madame de Pompadour to her favourite architect, Jean Cailleteau.

42

She thought she could see an open box of Debauve et Gallais chocolates, but it was only a box of jewellery.

43

Is it because Shakespeare, Marlowe and Racine were ignorant of chocolates that they wrote such enduring tragedies?

44

Through any trepidation the surest, safest, stepping-stones are chocolates.

45

CHOCOLATES-ON-THE-SOFA PHASE: The phase some women go through following the break-up of a relationship. Quantities of chocolates are consumed while sitting in the comfort of a sofa, perhaps with a large teddy bear in attendance. A form of self-therapy, the hope – not unjustified – is for the mysterious potency of chocolates to work like a healing balm, dissolving the pangs of separation and lifting the emotions from their gloom.

46

From the assimilation of good chocolates comes the suffusion of what Jonathan Swift said were the two noblest things in life: sweetness and light.

47

CHOCOPHARMACOLOGY: The study of the active ingredients in chocolate and their effects on the mind and body. As an advert for Radio 4 once put it: 'Often people get palpitations, euphoria, increased hormone secretions. It's a very strong substance, chocolate'.

48

In her bestselling book *Why Women Need Chocolate*, Debra Waterhouse records that chocolate contains more brain-pleasing chemicals than any other foodstuff. Research, interviews and anecdotes all concur: chocolate is a great comforter, a non-drug mood-enhancer, second only to sex, as good as sex, *even better* than sex.

49

Some chocolates are so tempting, just looking at them, or just thinking about them, creates the desired pharmacological effect.

50

If chocolates are the illness they are also the remedy.

51

At last they found the missing piece to the jigsaw: it was a caramelized butter ganache from La Maison du Chocolat, as silky as a newly opened Hermès scarf.

52

Apodictically, there are no such entities as funereal chocolates.

53

When it comes to expensive chocolates of quality, the border between luxury and necessity is very ill-defined.

54

CHOCOSCOPOPHILIA: The fondness for looking at, or for writing about, the opulence of chocolates.

55

CHOCOLATERIE: Not just an elegant shop in which quality chocolates are sold but, with its marble counter and *de luxe* wood cabinetry, also an embassy of style in which the liveried attendants are ambassadors of taste.

56

CHOCOLATE HEAVEN: The blissful state similar to being in two *chocolateries* at the same time.

57

At the moment of its deglutition a chocolate is a voluptuous deluge of affirmations. As Voltaire said, 'It is not a small thing to give pleasure'.

58

The pleasure of a ganache is perfect to begin with, and then gets better.

59

Some ganaches can move mountains. Some ganaches *are* mountains.

60

GLISSADE CHOCOLATIQUE: The slow and sybaritic consumption of chocolates – a degustation smoother than a sleigh ride in Switzerland.

61

A chocolate should also be seen as a miniature gâteau, so that one can say, 'O! how the diminution becomes it'.

62

In the search for hidden joys leave no chocolate unturned.

63

And once consumed a chocolate will metamorphose irrevocably into poetry.

64

A chocolate is a flourish on the portals of speech.

65

Stand in Venice, like Byron, on the Bridge of Sighs –
an almond ganache in each hand.

66

The hand that holds a ganache also holds your heart.

67

'From my room to the moon is thousands of miles,
Or a handmade chocolate and one of your smiles.'

68

'Last night I dreamt Louise
    Was eating chocolates to appease
The longing in her heart
    That we should never be apart.'

69

Chocolates have all the doors for poetry to make its entrance.

70

CHOCOLEPSY: The yearning to have, or to be near, chocolates. In 2002, when Fortnum & Mason placed an advert for a new chocolate buyer, someone willing to travel the world to select the best chocolate for the company's clientele, they were inundated with over 3,000 applications, including one from the personnel manager's nine year-old daughter.

71

Moderation is a virtue only in those who do not like pralines, cocoa-dusted truffles, giandujas, ganaches, crèmes, caramels, rochers, orangettes, croquants, liqueurs, palets d'or, chocolate-covered coffee beans, and expensive single-estate chocolate bars.

72

In the thraldom of a chocolate the two halves are bigger than the whole.

73

Is an attraction to chocolates an affection, or is it an affliction?

74

To say that chocolates are addictive is to understate the matter – they are positively alluring.

75

CHOCOPHAGOUS: Feeding on chocolates. Those who dine on heavenly foods such as lavender ganaches, cinnamon pralines, and butter mocha cups have no need of mortal sustenance.

76

Smooth and chaste like porcelain, the delicate face of a chocolate never knows the bitter taste of tears.

77

Why ask for the moon when you can have a praline, made with roasted Catalonian almonds and Tuscan hazelnuts, and dipped in the smoothest, tastiest milk chocolate?

78

Chocolates are the currency of love. The more it is used the more its value increases. So spend it, encourage it, distribute it as widely as possible, until the world is choc-full of its luscious coinage.

79

Pralines and ganaches are the first refuge of the incurably voluptuous.

80

It is the duty of nobility to oblige with chocolates, but has any aristocrat been more obligingly noble than Baron Alphonse de Rothschild who, in his will of 1905, left 25,000 gold francs to his son-in-law Albert, 'so that he might buy himself some chocolates'?

81

The marvel of chocolates is how such a rich diversity of tastes and textures is created from the marriage of such polar opposites: the sweetness of sugar and the bitterness of cocoa.

82

Chocolates have all the flavours of fervours.

83

Build ziggurats of pralines!

84

The best that chocolates have to give us is in the enthusiasm they inspire.

85

If it's too good to be true it's good enough to be a ganache from La Maison du Chocolat.

86

Can any other mortal mixture breathe such divine enchanting ravishment as a ganache?

87

In the astronomy of gastronomy all the stars are *grand cru* chocolates.

88

CHOCOTONAL: A voice that sounds like chocolate. The richness of singer Karen Carpenter's voice was described as bitterness dipped in chocolate; and it was said of soul legend Barry White that his deep, velvety voice sounded like chocolate fudge cake.

89

Whether milk, dark, flavoured or plain, every chocolate has its own character but in each one there is a little of all of us.

90

Ye who seek to perpetuate love and friendship: how wide is your experience, and how deep is your knowledge, of chocolates?

91

The greatest skill worth acquiring is knowing how to protract a chocolate.

92

The reward for those who have loved chocolates for a long time is to love them for all time.

93

Having found a layer of crunchy hazelnut praliné atop a caramelized almond base, it follows that many more delicious dimensions of pleasure will be found.

94

With its smooth flowing surfaces incorporating attractive features of interest, a chocolate is the kind of simple elegant harmony that keeps angels smiling and lovers loving.

95

Let us smile with the rich and eat chocolates with the beautiful.

96

To some, chocolate is more than just food, it has its own personality and develops relationships with those who love it. It is intimate, mysterious, complex and versatile. Some say it is masculine, others say it is feminine. It is neither, yet it is both. Consumers campaign for it to be classified as a separate food group. In short, chocolate is human.

97

CHOCOLATRY: The adoration of chocolates. Have you venerated a chocolate today?

98

Although it is advisable to eat fresh cream ganaches within a few days of purchase, it is even better to eat a few within a day of purchase.

99

CHOCOLACIOUS: Salaciously delicious.

100

Those who eat after-dinner mints late at night should not be surprised if they wake up after eight.

101

Verily, in the magnanimous moment of a chocolate all our shortcomings are mitigated.

102

CHOCOLATE BOX PARADOX: The more chocolates there are to choose from the more difficult it is to choose. Fortunately this paradox is also a fallacy.

103

All because the lady loves chocolates like Michel Cluizel's croquant, gianduja, crunchy hazelnut praliné, and single-origin dark chocolate ganaches.

104

If music is the food of love, chocolates such as these are the musicians.

105

Select chocolates that are, at least, worthy of your respect. Adventurous, even. Chocolates that are *considerate* – that would have the decency to wait for you in the street, waiting to help you if you lost your way; or wait for you in the bedroom, hoping to enter your dreams.

106

All desires eventually return to chocolates.

107

It is tempting to apply to chocolates the dictum in Rabelais' *Gargantua*: 'The appetite grows by eating'.

108

Or Mark Antony's comment in *Antony and Cleopatra*: 'She makes hungry where most she satisfies'.

109

As the poet Wallace Stevens almost put it: I do not know which to prefer, the beauty of form or the beauty of composition; eating a praline or just after.

110

Caramel – a humble flavour that is crowned with splendour when coated in chocolate.

111

Nougatines – pediments of our sweetest sentiments.

112

The best way to eat a ganache is to let it slowly deliquesce on the tongue like a communion wafer.

113

Chocolates are so much more enjoyable when eaten in private, particularly if that privacy is threatened.

114

Of all the pulchritudinous profiles of plenitude chocolates are the puckers of paradise – rosebuds for the tastebuds.

115

'These violet delights lead to violet ends.'

– *Friar Lawrence's comment on Charbonnel et Walker's violet creams?*

116

REVERBERANT RESEARCH (1): A study by American psychologists at the University of Pennsylvania concluded that people eat chocolate because . . . they like it!

117

Eating chocolates is like eating cherries – first we pick the best ones then we end up eating them all.

118

The apperception of her face across the street – how many chocolates could taste as sweet?

119

If you are looking for another occasion to have chocolates, provide the chocolates and you will have found the occasion.

120

The best dinner parties are those at which the chocolates are served first. What follows is simply superfluous.

121

There is no need to trifle with desserts when there are truffles to consider.

122

'Taste, aroma, size, shape, sensation – these are the feathers that give all good chocolates their *mmmmm* wings of flight.'

– From a letter by Madame de Pompadour who, in all her years at court, was never known to tell a lie.

123

D'ARCY'S LAW OF CHOCOLATE CONSUMPTION: That appetite always increases to meet the quantity of chocolates available. Thus, no matter how many milk or dark chocolates there are in a box, they will inevitably be consumed within a shorter time than expected.

124

When women are happy and fortunate they buy champagne, chocolates and flowers. When men are happy and fortunate *they* buy champagne, chocolates and flowers.

125

Is there any other way a woman may be more profitably engaged than in eating her way through a box of expensive chocolates?

126

In their laughter some women have the sound of handmade cocoa-dusted truffles tumbling like lottery balls.

127

It is almost the definition of an elegant lady that she never imposes on someone eating a chocolate.

128

THE CHOCOLATE HORIZON: The level of volition in the desire for a chocolate which, once exceeded, cannot be reversed.

129

Ah, soft centres – so hard to resist. So hard to resist.

130

It is a good eater who makes a good chocolate even better.

131

Like satin slippers, chocolates come best in pairs.

132

CHOCOLATIC: The description of a person who is as pleasing to the senses as chocolates are: a beautiful woman with lovely chocolate-brown hair; a well-loved singer, model or actor with dark, chocolatey skin; heart-throbs like Johnny Depp or Brad Pitt who, to their fans, are 'forever yummy'; Mr Darcy, and the heroes of so many romantic novels.

133

AXIOM OF UNITY: A man and a woman are one. A man, a woman, and a Debauve et Gallais chocolate are one.

134

One man is as good as another until he has eaten a Michel Cluizel plum marmalade ganache.

135

In the black and white world of dinner suits chocolates are the rainbows of gastronomy.

136

On the brink of satiation some chocolates appear to have no end.

137

Chocolates like these are such stuff as dreams are made on.

138

Do not say 'a chocolate' and dismiss it with casual familiarity, but see it for the first time as a newly encountered love who has yet to be kissed.

139

A chocolate is only a chocolate until it is tasted, then it is a salutation to the senses.

140

CHOCOLALIA: The sensual, lingual vocabulary of chocolate appreciation, and the phraseology of its expression: 'velvety mouthfeel', 'meltingly soft', 'intensely silky', 'smoothly finished', etc.

141

Chocolates encapsulate the delights of poetry, music and flowers to eclipse them all.

142

ROMEO: 'O! that I were a gold-wrapped gianduja that she might hold me in her hand.'

143

'If poets dream of the chocolates his mouth rhymes, When lovers steal his smiles are these crimes?'

– *Epigram found in the margin of one of Madame de Pompadour's poetry books.*

144

THE MILK TRAY APPROACH: Taking its name from the TV adverts in which a daredevil James Bond-type risks waterfalls, cliffs and sharks etc. to bring his lady a box of chocolates, the Milk Tray Approach is the romantic interpretation of chocolates: all rose petals, soft lighting, *Rhapsody in Blue*, and more than a whiff of sex.

145

Because chocolates appeal to all the senses they are never far from the Milk Tray Approach, which is why they are often used as code for sex, especially in Valentine's Day messages: 'Charlie come back to bed and bring the choccies'; 'Chocolate boy be mine'; and, 'Only some dark chocolates but all my love'.

146

Phonetically 'chocolate' is imitative of coursing water. Like water for chocolate, about to overflow with passion.

147

And, significantly, in pronouncing the word 'chocolate' the lips are pouted as if to kiss.

148

No doubt if Rodin were alive today he would carve *The Kiss* wholly out of chocolate.

149

CHOCOLAGRAM: An anagram which reveals Milk Tray intentions concealed in a brand or variety of chocolates. A chocolagram is a peek under the bedclothes, as it were, to find out who, or what, is lying underneath:

A Chocolate Orange = *Echo to a carnal ego*
Leonidas coffee praline = *Nice ladies peel off, Rona*
Godiva selection = *A coveted soiling*
Lindt Selection = *O! still indecent*
After Eights = *Great fetish*
Suchard Evocations = *Each diva's contours*
Cadbury's Milk Tray = *A busty lady, Mr Rick?*
Prestat creams = *M.'s a pert actress*
Bendicks of Mayfair = *OK, I fancy M.'s fair bed*
Thornton's Continental = *Lo! instant horn content*
Green and Black's = *Neck, legs and bra*
Cocoa-dusted = *Adds a cute coo*
Black Magic chocolates = *Catholic comeback slag*
Neapolitans = *No panties, Al.*
Thickly enrobed = *Be tickled horny*
A Terry's All Gold = *Grr! Sell to a lady*
Joël Durand = *A nude Lord J.*
Praline hearts = *At/near her lips*
Gourmet truffles = *Lures R. to get muff*
Dark liqueur cup = *A quick, rude slur*
Hand decorated = *Dead hot dancer*
Nestlé Dairy Box = *A sexily torn bed*

150

Cupid's quiver is content to be empty of arrows as long as it is full of chocolates.

151

Chocolates are both the fuel and the fire.

152

Love in her long dress finds words too tight, but a ganache is a flouncy skirt in which she can flirt with ease.

153

THE ENSELLURE TEST: The test in which a lover is judged by whether or not one would enjoy eating truffles from their *ensellure* – the cup-like depression in the small of the back.

154

The satin ribbons, tissue layers, and little frilly cups inform us that, in its symbolism, chocolate packaging inhabits the same emotional hinterland as lingerie: we are invited to 'undress' our chocolates before arriving at the sweetness underneath.

155

ROMEO: 'I am no pilot yet were your truffles as far as that vast shore wash'd with the farthest sea, I would adventure for such a merchandise.'

156

JULIET: 'O! I have bought the mansion of a love and filled it with truffles to die for.'

157

She served the chocolates in one of her lacy bras. If only she had had fuller breasts . . .

158

Caparison the caramel cups!

159

REVERBERANT RESEARCH (2): A survey conducted by the American Boxed Chocolates Manufacturers found 29% of men believed that giving their partner a box of chocolates improved their chances of getting sex in return.

160

Like a woman looking at a man with amorous intent, some chocolates are tasted with the whole heart, the whole mind, and the whole body.

161

CHOCOLIPS: The suggestively loaded slogans so prevalent in chocolate advertising, such as: 'Women finally get what they want'; 'Live your nights to the taste of dark chocolate'; 'Hand finished by Belgians'; and, 'Now with extra *mmm* and *ahh*'.

162

All thoughts of a chocolate in a single image, and the image is a mirror.

163

CHOCOLEXY: The popular notion of chocolates as aphrodisiacs. In George Orwell's *1984*, for example, Winston and Julia consume an illicit bar of 'dark and shiny' chocolate before consummating their secret passion; and in the series of short stories *Seduction by Chocolate*, four couples discover that chocolate is the catalyst, the sorcerer, the irresistible seducer who enchants them all.

164

Chocolexy is such a fundamental part of our relationship with chocolates it is difficult to imagine them without it.

165

Those keen to push the notion further have likened the eating of a chocolate liqueur to the sexual act itself.

166

Smooth, romantic, sialogogic – an Italian gigolo or an Italian gianduja?

167

'Chocolates are the piano keys on which I play the music of my life.'

– *Prince Metternich, Chancellor and Foreign Minister of the Austrian Empire, and gourmet chocolate lover.*

168

In the soft, creamy centre of a praline the palate finds the kindness and tenderness of a rose.

169

In the lexicon of truffles a *coryphée* is the type you can't have just one or two of, can't have just three or four of . . .

170

Sometimes a chocolate looks like a loving kiss, sometimes it looks like a sweet smile, and sometimes it is the sheer thrill of alternating between the two.

171

When a chocolate is admitted into the mouth the lips curve round it like the arms of two lovers embracing.

172

Chocolates are also a kind of *Kama Sutra*: laconical, canonical and gastronomical.

173

Is there a best time to feed your lover chocolates? First thing in the morning? Yes, antejentacular chocolates (from the Latin *ante*, before, and *ientaculum*, the first meal of the day). They wake you up and cocoa.

174

One woman is as seductive as another until she has eaten an ultra smooth ganache from La Maison du Chocolat.

175

Gadroon her ganaches!

176

Eloquence resides less in a woman's tone of voice and choice of words than in the way her lips move when eating a chocolate.

177

CHOCOLANDRIST: A woman who measures a man's attractiveness by whether or not he is worth his weight in chocolate – milk or dark, hard or soft.

178

It is an axiom that good chocolates, like women, will always find a way.

179

Was Plato alluding to the power of ganaches when he said, 'Appearance has more force than reality'?

180

Every chocolate has its depths to one who truly sees.

181

Like all great encounters the best chocolates can be appreciated three times over: in anticipation, in consumption, and in recollection.

182

Two lovers in bed together, one of them is eating chocolates. Does this constitute infidelity?

183

No man is an island but some women are cocoa-dusted truffles.

184

'In a praline heart you send me your Valentine,' said the dancer to his inamorata, 'I give you my answer in the first bite'.

185

PARFAIT: A woman who has beautiful light brown skin, smooth and shiny like Godiva pralines; dark hair tumbling down like lustrous French ganaches; and a smile sweeter than Charbonnel et Walker champagne truffles.

186

Sinful caramels, muffled truffles, erotic crèmes – ah, the women in men's most propitious dreams.

187

And who has not at some time fantasized about a fairytale princess, swathed in diaphanous chiffon, choosing chocolates from a crystal chalice?

188

Seduction is the ebb and flow of chocolates.

189

When lovers blanch, chocolates put the words back in their mouths.

190

To those for whom chocolates are wanton, who yearn for them, and who languish in their absence, the Milk Tray Approach is the *only* approach.

191

A woman *can* have too many handbags, if the handbags are not full of chocolates.

192

Is an adoration from afar the shadow of a chocolate we have felt, or of one we long to feel?

193

When judged by the senses, a ganache has more sonority than the heaviest philosophy.

194

CHOCOMANCY: The divination of a future lover's name by truffles and pralines. Letters of the alphabet are written down in a circle and a truffle or praline is placed over each one. As the first two or three chocolates are eaten, the letters so revealed prognosticate the initials of the lover.

195

Love is indeed a fortuitous chooser of chocolates.

196

CHOCOSOPHY: The wisdom of chocolates: a mind crenellated with truffles, ganaches and pralines.

197

Mix with your sage counsels fine foreign ganaches.

198

To be wise in life is not to forget the seductive power of pralines.

199

To be wise in *love* is not to forget the 'i' in kiss is dotted with a truffle.

200

A chocolate as dark as night can make your day.

201

Sometimes chocolates enter into our possession like keys we thought we had lost.

202

Or say that chocolates are keyholes through which we get glimpses of the heaven we will one day find.

203

The saints of our time are those who have been canonised by cocoa.

204

If ever your transgressions find you behind bars make sure they are *grand cru* chocolate bars.

205

A ganache, like love, is tentative at the beginning, exquisite in the middle, and endless at the end.

206

CHOCOCORE: The soft centre within us all. The painter John Constable called it the calm sunshine of the heart. It is an inner truffle that is there for life.

207

A lover's smile reverberates in the heart like pralines crepitating unseen.

208

CHOCOPHILE: Someone with a great love for, or an inordinate attraction to, chocolates. Chocophiles don't *buy* chocolates, they worship them at the altars of Theobroma; they don't *unwrap* chocolates, they undress them; and they don't just *eat* chocolates, they have passionate encounters with them.

209

Vienna, famous for its Sacher Torte and *fin de siècle* cafés with velvet seating and sumptuous chandeliers, is where the chocolates still waltz in and out of your dreams.

210

Paris, luminous city of culture and shrine of haute cuisine, is where the chocolates still cast shadows of the *Ancien Régime*.

211

Debauve et Gallais, the oldest *chocolaterie* in Paris, is where chocolates are displayed like guards of honour – in endless conjurations of chocolatude.

212

It was while admiring the Hall of Mirrors at the Palace of Versailles that, seeing her face reflected in the shiny surface of a praline, he felt he knew her properly for the first time.

213

'My greatest strength is that I am too weak to resist a chocolate.'

— A note found in Madame de Pompadour's prayer book.

214

Chocolates apprehend and preserve those ineffable moments of significance which emerge between events of great importance.

215

The greatest verity of extolment is that every chocolate has a purpose.

216

In the sequence of truffles, ardent felicity follows ardent delight.

217

CHOCOMANIA: The condition of being enthralled by chocolates. The fact that it cannot be cured should not necessarily be seen as cause for concern.

218

CHOCOLOGY: The study of chocolates. Every year, the combined weight of all the books written about chocolates is still less than the total weight of all the chocolates consumed.

219

I am a person of few words but 'chocolates' is one of them.

220

Some chocolates are so deep they say more in a nibble than can be said in a whole bite.

221

Whether they are square, conical, triangular or lozenged, it is in the nature of chocolates that they will go round.

222

Generosity will win favour with anyone, particularly when it is accompanied by a prize-winning ballotin of pralines.

223

Half a chocolate is often a whole pleasure.

224

CHOCOLATISATION: The harmonising and civilising influence of chocolates. Chocolatisation was first applied by the big chocolate manufacturers of the late nineteenth and early twentieth centuries when, under the benign influence of their confectionery, they were moved to provide employees with better wages, housing, healthcare and education.

225

It features in the novel *Chocolat*, where wounded relationships in a French village are healed with the help of cocoa nibs, chocolate seashells, Nipples of Venus, and scrumptious cups of spicy hot chocolate.

226

And during the filming of *Chocolat*, when relations on set were kept smooth by all the chocolate around.

227

And in 1996, when the authority responsible for the Paris Metro employed staff to hand out chocolates to passengers, as a bid to dissuade them from smoking.

228

And in 2002, when a group of anarchists accused of storming the Argentinian Embassy in London were set free at the end of their trial, because all they had done was distribute Ferrero Rochers to the staff.

229

As Scott of the Antarctic wrote in his journal: 'Crunching those elaborate chocolates brought one nearer to civilisation than anything we experienced'.

230

The language of rapture is written in chocolates.

231

It is not just kind, civilised people who give chocolates but, in giving chocolates people are made kinder and more civilised.

232

When all is said and done, chocolates still have more to say and do.

233

CHOCOLATUDE: The cultural and poetic values of chocolates – a soft, curvaceous ambit ranging from crinolines and kisses, to palaces, peace and pergolas.

234

Some chocolates are so precious they could be weighed in carats.

235

CHOCOMEN: An omen that foretells a chocolate. A nightingale singing with full-throated ease foretells a milk chocolate soon to be melting on the palate; a black cat crossing one's path foretells a dark chocolate soon to be crossing one's lips.

236

There is no better way to fill the gaps in one's education than with chocolates – they are the books that show, contain and nourish the world.

237

CHOCOSCOPY: Interpreting the world through chocolate-tinted spectacles. Chocoscopy asks of *Tender is the Night* whether it was the night that was tender or the chocolates; and of *Pride and Prejudice*, it wonders whether Elizabeth's heart would not have melted sooner if Mr Darcy had had the foresight to present her with an agreeable box of rose creams.

238

In *Remembrance of Things Past* Proust recounts how the eating of a madeleine cake filled him with 'exquisite pleasure', triggering a host of coruscating memories. How much more coruscating might these memories have been had the trigger been a ganache?

239

When Baudelaire wrote, 'Here there is nothing but order and beauty, luxury, calm and pleasure', did he know that, on a street not far away, a branch of La Maison du Chocolat would one day be opened?

240

Regarding the Mona Lisa: on the reason for her enigmatic smile the art world has been deliberating for centuries. Perhaps she had just eaten a ganache?

241

I wonder what chocolates have to say about us?

242

Moonlight on a solitary chocolate and do we not see a precious figurine in the night?

243

The most inspiring prospect a person ever sees is an open box of chocolates.

244

'Conveying a sense of tradition in an expressive beauty of composition and form that is wholly its own, every chocolate is an icon.'

– *A note found in Madame de Pompadour's* Moll Flanders.

245

It is an axiom that sooner or later we find chocolates.

246

There are ganaches so exquisite all they lack are the pedestals on which to mount them.

247

Fabergé chocolates – what an exuberant concept!

248

One chocolate properly known and understood is enough to reveal all the glories of love and life.

249

Ah, the polyphony of chocolates!

250

With ganaches, enough is not always enough.

251

A ballotin is a library of chocolates.

252

CHOCOLIT: Literature that reads like chocolate: not necessarily *about* chocolate, but redolent of it. For some, it's books such as the *Harry Potter* series, described by Stephen Fry as 'like swimming in chocolate', or romantic fiction in general; for others it's the lush, erotic tales of Laurell K. Hamilton which read 'like dark chocolate with hints of expresso and orange peel'. And then there are books like the inspirational *Chocolate for Women* stories, written to caress the heart and nourish the soul.

253

The word 'chocolates' may not rhyme with many other words, but many rhymes are other words for chocolates.

254

Chocolate thoughts in a blue mind – where the eager imagination begins.

255

Bitter chocolates leave such sweet memories.

256

For every chocolate there is an insight.

257

CHOCOGLYPH: A phrasal image of chocolatude, such as: 'sweet inspiration', 'cream believer', or 'soft-centred'. Chocoglyphs can be abstract or precise, reflective or descriptive, but always with those beguiling elements of luxury, pleasure and indulgence so characteristic of chocolates. They stand out from the text around them like opals in bedrock.

258

It is always reassuring to encounter chocoglyphs in the pages of a novel.

259

A chocolate is a concise dictionary of pleasures in which words such as 'devastation' are not found.

260

As La Rochefoucauld almost put it: felicity dwells in taste and not in things; we are happy through having the chocolates we enjoy, and not through having the chocolates others deem enjoyable.

261

All the charm of the Muses flowing in a single word, and the word is chocolates, chocolates, chocolates.

262

If Keats were alive today he would die for a box of violet creams.

263

To connect the moment with sweetness – that is the purpose of a chocolate.

264

Flowers say it occasionally, but chocolates say it all the time: life is sweet and we were born to enjoy it.

265

Whose fondant hearts are softer than mousse, mallow English maidens cluster like nuts round the rose creams looking for cuddly bears.

266

A nightingale sang in Berkeley Square but nobody heard it. They were too busy admiring the hostess's chocolate shoes. Unforgettable.

267

Chocolates do ornament a bedroom.

268

Thousands of people were celebrating in Paris's Avenue de Messine, but the only movement in the crowd was from a woman's chocolate-brown eyes.

269

Birds of a feather flock to eat chocolates together.

270

CHOCISM: A management maxim with a chocolate theme:

1. It's OK to think outside the box as long as it's not outside the chocolate box.
2. One cannot say there is ever an absence of chocolates, only that sometimes one is in the wrong place.
3. Live for the moment. For the moment it takes to think of chocolates; for the moment it takes to buy chocolates; and for the moment it takes to eat a chocolate.

271

Those with the best advice offer chocolates.

272

A butterfly alighting on a book of poetry; rose petals sprinkled on damask sheets; a praline proximate to expectant lips – these are the arbours of quiescence which give rhetoric its repose.

273

CHOCOPATHY: When the world is reduced to one thing – chocolates. Chocopathy links everything, however tenuously, to figurative or literal qualities of chocolates. It connects, for example, the basque – the lacy female undergarment – to Basque, the province in SW France, because it was in this region that French chocolate was first manufactured.

274

And who would quibble with ribbons, bows, and a thousand days of chocolates as an image of peace?

275

CHOCOLETTE: An epitome of chocolate opulence, as in: 'He waved at the paintings, mirrors, brocades and *boulle* furniture around him, and said, "I only bought all this so I could enjoy my ganaches in the proper surroundings: every gem should have a worthy setting" '.

276

Or in: 'Her gaze panned across the Grand Hall, from a balustrade of *verde antico* marble to a painting of Euterpe, Muse of music and pleasure. As her attention lingered on this eighteenth century allegory she realised – O salutations to synchronicity – that the Muse was holding a double flute with the same affectionate solicitude with which she herself was holding a box of Fortnum & Mason chocolates'.

277

If you want another image of opulence, picture a classic silk-lined Louis Vuitton suitcase filled to the brim with gift-wrapped ballotins of pralines.

278

Or a butler polishing the after-dinner mints before they are served. Or chocolates delivered in a Landau.

279

If it's monuments you require, would you consider an entablature of Valrhona couverture?

280

CHOCOSPHERE: An environment of chocolatude – beauty and opulence in sumptuous surroundings; a haven of serenity; a place of inspiration and renewal.

281

There are images enough in a single chocolate to sustain a lifetime of reveries. They are the nipples of providence.

282

Listen to the triumphal second movement of Beethoven's Fifth Piano Concerto, the *Emperor*. Do you not hear a faithful similitude of the elation felt on opening a box of Debauve et Gallais chocolates?

283

Ah, the tempting tintinnabulation of truffles.

284

Smooth, graceful, neo-classical, a praline is only a praline until it is seen, then it is an *objet d'art*.

285

A chocolate is a kind of transubstantiation – the manifestation of a sweet inspiration.

286

CHOCOLATION: The blissful anticipation when in close proximity to chocolates, or the anticipation of chocolates when in close proximity to something blissful. As when reading a *Miss Read* book, where even the most jaded reader feels as though she is skipping through a summer meadow in a negligée pursued by Jude Law throwing violet creams at her.

287

Bring me my arrows of desire, but first dip them in rich, single-estate chocolate.

288

In the summit of heaven, sweet-tongued in satin boxes, delicious chocolates never demur, never shut their eyes.

289

Chocolates are the tropes and trophies of our epicurean adventures.

290

'A chocolate is a refuge in which harm cannot occur, and where perfection stands apart from the corrosive power of weakness and time.'

– *From a letter written by Madame de Pompadour to François Boucher.*

291

A chocolate is the apotheosis of a cocoa bean.

292

'Hail ye small sweet courtesies of life.'

– *Laurence Sterne's 18th century address to chocolates?*

293

That love is sweet is incontestable, but it is a delight we owe to the perpetual pleasure of chocolates.

294

CHOCOPHONIC: Containing, or reminiscent of, the tones of chocolatude. In the photo caption, 'Tsarina Feodorovna treasure-hunting in the gardens of Livadia', do we not picture an image of the Tsarina treasure-hunting for chocolates?

295

And in the susceptive swish of a satin dress down a marble staircase, or in the tap, tap, tap of stiletto heels on parquet flooring, do we not hear the prelude to a box of Hédiard chocolates?

296

CHOCOMORPHIC: Shaped like a chocolate. Like the grand châteaux of the Loire, shapes that are perfectly proportioned and harmonious, perfectly elegant and imposing, and perfectly beautiful to behold.

297

In its shape, size and texture a chocolate combines practicality with pleasure to give us the perfect delectation.

298

If a chocolate is a symbol it can also be a clash of cymbals.

299

It is not just the thought that counts but how many chocolates one can count.

300

The formula for chocolates is: one more than the one before.

301

Constantly ebullient is the language of chocolates: whereas bottles of champagne are being uncorked somewhere in the world every two seconds, boxes of chocolates are being opened all the time.

302

THE SYMMETRY PRINCIPLE: That the conclusion to a chocolate may well be another chocolate.

303

The seasons come and go but the reasons for having chocolates will never change.

304

Lo! a little chocolate but a large joy.

305

CHOCOLATE IMPERATIVE: The chocolate aesthetic informing art, design, music and poetry. In art it can be seen in Elizabeth Vigée-Lebrun's *Self-Portrait with a Straw Hat* – those rustic flowers, that dashing ostrich feather, that milky *décolletage*; in design it can be seen in the celebratory motifs of the Rococo – all those fanciful curves and exuberant fronds; in music it can be heard in Tchaikovsky's *The Nutcracker* – in the charm of those scintillating folk dances; and in poetry it is at work in Keats' odes – those pastoral idylls, that lyricism, that nightingale!

306

CHOCODOXY: The belief that all art is chocolate: that the Gothic is bars of chocolate; the Baroque and the Rococo are pralines; the Romantic is dark chocolate assortments (the secret of the Black Magic box?); High Victorian Romanticism is so resonant with chocolatude that one can almost reach out and eat it; Impressionism is all ganaches (the cream, the light!); Portraiture is chocolate liqueurs; Cubism is broken chocolate pieces; Realism is thick, plain chocolate; Surrealism is chocolate fountains; Pop Art is molded chocolate shapes; and Conceptual Art is the wrapping.

307

CHOCOLITH: A sculpture in chocolate, usually celebratory, often symbolising the subject is good enough to eat, or commenting on notions of temporality, sensuality and consumption – like the chocolate flowers and dresses specially created for the yearly *Salon du Chocolat*.

308

One day you will fall asleep on a chaise longue – very Regency, dear – and wake up in a deep ballotin of Neuhaus pralines.

309

The best-loved sentence in the language of chocolates? 'Have another one.'

310

A chocolate is all the promise of a premise.

311

CHOCOLADITE: A chocolate dweller. The poet Coleridge used to dream of finding a mountain of plum cake and eating out rooms for himself to live in. If he were alive today he would dream of hollowing out a chocolate to live in.

312

These days, chocoladites rent or buy properties close to their favourite wish fulfilment.

313

A room with a view is a room with a tureen full of truffles.

314

To conscientiously acquaint oneself with the aesthetics of chocolate refines one's behaviour and prevents it from becoming coarse.

315

CHOCOLATIST. A collector of chocolate curios – cufflinks, lipsticks, coffee cups, etc. – personal and household possessions rendered all the more poignant by not being exactly fit for purpose.

316

Diamonds are forever – forever dreaming of being chocolates.

317

Whoever said the best things in life are free was obviously not a lover of top quality chocolates.

318

DEIPNOSOPHY: The art of intelligent table talk: the harvest of news, pleasantries and opinions reaped from a timely sowing of expensive chocolates.

319

When the stars talk of childbirth they mean a white fondant centre being born in heaven.

320

Life begins at forty. Forty chocolates in a box.

321

CHOCOLISTIC: The comparison of life to a box of chocolates, as in: 'Life is a box of chocolates – you never know when you're going to get a fudge'. Because life *is* a box of chocolates: we are born when the box is opened; we live as we choose our way through the assortment; and we die when the box is empty.

322

CHOCOSTASIS: The mental equilibrium, the physical state of relaxation, which follows the assimilation of chocolates.

323

It is an observation, perhaps a profundity, that life is a dance in which we move only in order to preserve the stillness of a chocolate.

324

Love is a lily, or even a tempest, but a chocolate is a cynosure.

325

REVERBERANT RESEARCH (3): What is it about chocolate mints that they should seal the deals? A 1990's survey on corporate buyers of Bendicks mints found that stockbrokers had a zeal for the slim Mayfair Mints; fund managers went weak at the knees for the robust Bittermints; equity salesmen had a penchant for the crunchy Mint Crisps; and gilt brokers melted for the gooey Crème de Menthes.

326

In my bold opinion, if Madame de Pompadour's most favoured artist, François Boucher, were alive today he would be designing nothing but beautiful chocolate boxes.

327

During the early twentieth century, the notorious dancer and seductress Mati Hari was known for her affair with the French chocolate magnate Gaston Ménier. She must have known . . .

328

CHOCOLATEER: A soldier proffering chocolates for peace, a chocolate soldier, the most well-known example of which is the Swiss mercenary in *Arms and the Man* who, instead of carrying cartridges in battle, carried chocolates instead. Perhaps it was he who inspired Queen Victoria to dispatch 100,000 tins of chocolate to her troops fighting in the Boer War?

329

Since then, chocolateers have been present in every significant military conflict. In 1914 chocolateers appeared during the unofficial Christmas truce on the Western Front, when British, French and German troops exchanged gifts of chocolate in the fond hope that hostilities would not be resumed.

330

In 1944, following their sweep through France after D-Day, US soldiers handed out chocolate to the newly liberated citizens of Paris – chocolate which, according to one grateful female recipient, was so good the taste was never forgotten.

331

In 2003, the US government dismissed the countries proposing a separate military command to NATO as mere 'chocolate makers'. Was the US government afraid that France, Belgium, Germany and Luxembourg were creating a new precedent for European peace – an army of chocolate soldiers? If so, why did the American military develop its own special beige, brown and tan camouflage known as 'chocolate-chip camouflage'?

332

Chocolates are the patriotism of the peaceful.

333

Say either:
1. That life is a parcelling out of time into chocolates; or,
2. That time is a parcelling out of life into chocolates.

334

As Marcus Aurelius might have put it: make the rules of your life brief, but deep enough to embrace the fundamentals of chocolates; recurrence to them will then suffice to remove all vexations.

335

The best that chocolates have to give us is in the memories they leave behind.

336

Assuredly, a quiet, unhurried ganache is an island of silence in a sea of shouts.

337

It is so quiet you can hear a chocolate drop.

338

Fullness is an empty box of chocolates.

339

CHOCOGEOGRAPHY: The description of the earth's natural features in terms of chocolate. In Canada there is a Chocolate Lake and a Chocolate River; in America there is a Chocolate Bay and a Chocolate Mountain; in the Philippines there are Chocolate Hills; and in Wales there is even a Chocolate Farm.

340

In the *Sailor's Wordbook* of 1867 a 'chocolate-gale' was defined as a brisk NW wind in the West Indies, so-called because it churned the sea a chocolatey-brown colour. Or was it because when the wind blew the Captain would distribute chocolates to his crew as a means of assuaging their fear?

341

Night is a dark truffle the day devours at dawn.

342

CHOCOLATE CITY: A city whose architecture and cultural heritage make it the perfect backdrop to the consumption of chocolates: Paris, Vienna, Geneva, Venice, Prague, and Brussels are all chocolate cities of note, especially Brussels, where almost every *rue* and *avenue* has its own elegant *chocolaterie*.

343

CHOCAMULET: A chocolate with protective powers, such as the Bendicks Bittermint one customer used to keep in the pocket of his waistcoat – a talisman to be reached for, and held on to, in times of danger.

344

Assuredly, somewhere, at sometime, chocolates like these are seeking your kind solicitation.

345

Whereas a chandelier is a pretty petticoat of lights, a chocolate is a sumptuous robe of rapture.

346

'What would life be to us if truffles were no more? Would we feel night behind us, darker than before?'

347

Like a painting before it's painted, a chocolate before it's eaten.

348

'The clavichord of my heart has been tuned and I am ready to sing the praises of your chocolates.'

— *From a letter written by Madame de Pompadour.*

349

Was it the rumbling of distant timpani or the tumbling of nearby truffles?

350

Treat a chocolate with respect and it will become your friend. Treat it as a friend and it will become your lover.

351

Naturally a crunchy hazelnut *bâton* would rather be a million than a mullion.

352

Sometimes chocolates are only the notes. At other times they are the symphony itself.

353

CASCADE SYSTEM: The way in which, when eating chocolates, the first stimulates the desire for the second, the second stimulates the desire for the third, the third stimulates the desire for the fourth, and so on until the entire box has been consumed.

354

Happiness is a copious supply of chocolates and an endless appetite.

355

Food for the gods or food from the gods?

356

Gold, frankincense, myrrh. And the fourth wise man brought a ballotin of pralines.

357

INCREDIBLES: Chocolates so beautiful they can be seen even when the eyes are closed – like Debauve et Gallais' dark nougatine truffles, made with roasted Spanish almonds cooked in caramelized sugar, and wrapped in jewel-like pink foil.

358

Diamonds may be a girl's best friend but chocolates make sweeter companions.

359

A kiss is a chocolate at the moment of its inception.

360

In an ideal world the Royal Mint would also be responsible for the chocolate mints.

361

The cogs in my mind are turning, and they are Bendicks Bittermints.

362

A chocolate is also a sugar cube dreaming of Venice.

363

Ah! to sleep, perchance to dream of waking up in a branch of La Maison du Chocolat.

364

Desire makes the heart grow fonder but chocolates make the heart grow stronger.

365

REVERBERANT RESEARCH (4): A study published in the journal *Science News* showed that among ballerinas chocolate is a fetish food – it is always being thought about, talked about, and even dreamed about.

366

A *pas de deux* is the dance of a ballerina's attention from one chocolate to another as her mind makes the difficult decision of which to choose.

367

A diva is a coloratura chocolate.

368

'The elegance, the finesse, the subtlety of their shapes and textures, the combination of wit and gallantry in just the right proportions, give all good chocolates those qualities of poise and vivacity that people of taste find so agreeable.'

– *Note in a leather-bound journal found in Madame de Pompadour's boudoir.*

369

Happiness is also an after-dinner mint: prodigiously zestful but not without propriety.

370

A gentleman is as good as his word as long as the word is 'ganache'.

371

CHOCOFFENDER: Someone who breaks the law to obtain chocolates. In 2001, thieves in Lancashire stole two pallets' worth of Milk Tray from a storage depot. Although the crime was loudly condemned in the press at the time, the greatest opprobrium was saved for the tactless way in which the chocolates were secreted onto the black market, rather than into the bedrooms of the thieves' girlfriends.

372

They give twice who give chocolates.

373

LUSCIOUS DEBUT (1): 'If I were to chose my most preferred truffle you would be the one.'

374

LUSCIOUS DEBUT (2): He felt her presence to be like a box of Fouquet chocolates about to be opened.

375

When companies such as Thorntons can sell an *Eden* range featuring chocolates called Lust, Obsession and Desire, and companies such as Godiva can be named after an icon of female nudity, 'so that the legacy may be long remembered', is there any doubt as to the seductive Milk Tray intentions imbedded in boxed chocolates?

376

PERTINENT OBSERVATION: The bigger the box of chocolates, the bigger is the expectation in return. When London's notorious Windmill Theatre closed down in 1964, shops in Soho sold out of their biggest boxes of chocolates, which were being bought as gifts for the theatre's lovely dancing girls.

377

Slice a chocolate delicately like a peach; eat it on a plate with a dessert knife and fork; treat it as a course on its own and it will become a whole meal.

378

It is not enough to buy chocolates, one must also know how to eat them.

379

To fully appreciate chocolates it is recommended that you are in a relaxed state of mind and that your surroundings are suitably conducive.

380

There is hardly any unhappiness that will not be dissipated on opening a box of Amedei truffles.

381

When it comes to chocolates of significance the cost is insignificant.

382

My vacillating mind is now resolute – there is only one truffle left in the box.

383

If a picture is worth a thousand words, a chocolate is worth a thousand pictures.

384

One could so easily lose oneself in a Michel Cluizel ganache.

385

A chocolate is a heartbeat falling in love.

386

MEMORIALS: Following a spiritual experience in 1654, French philosopher Blaise Pascal recorded the vision in a private note to himself which he then carefully sewed into his coat, and transferred it when wearing lighter clothes in the summer. Known as the Memorial, Pascal's idea has inspired chocophiles ever since to inscribe their favourite chocolate quotations, and sew them into their clothes too.

387

In a chocolate there is room for everything.

388

It is so often an image of oneself that one sees reflected in a praline.

389

REVERBERANT RESEARCH (5): The *Atlas of Finite Simple Groups*, culminated after several decades of exploration, classifies the basic building blocks of the universe in terms of symmetries, or harmonies, and is the mathematicians' equivalent of the chemists' Periodic Table. Appropriately, the first symmetry to be classified is the example found in Escher's design for a chocolate box.

390

Seventh heaven is the seventh chocolate.

391

Memorably for the advancement of the Milk Tray Approach, in the 1970's Cadbury's increased their sales of Flake by wrapping it in phallic associations; and Fry's promoted their exaggeratedly pink Turkish Delight by hinting at something soft and feminine, 'full of Eastern promise'.

392

While, a few years later, in an upmarket brothel in London's South Kensington, contraceptives were kept in a chocolate tin. The girls obviously knew...

393

Even master *chocolatier* Robert Linxe, who pioneered the elevation of chocolates to the status of haute cuisine, incorporates Milk Tray elements in his chocolates: his solid, dark brown boxes may have a sober, masculine appeal, but the names of his famous ganaches are inspired by operatic themes and therefore wholly consistent with the seductive Milk Tray Approach.

394

A kiss is a search from lip to lip, from mouth to mouth, looking for the meaning of cocoa.

395

CHOCOLASMIA: Ornate or flowery prose sensuously evocative of chocolates. Charles Ryder in *Brideshead Revisited*, for example, 'drowning in honey, stingless'; or the philosopher-duke in *Venus Observed* seeing 'no end to the parcelling out of heaven in little beauties'.

396

Purple prose is chocolate prose. We should truffle and praline . . .

397

'I cannot imagine life without chocolate, it would be dreadful if there were none.'

– *TV presenter Valerie Singleton. In echo of every woman's attitude to chocolate?*

398

She waited at the station until the milk chocolates came . . . on a train of thought.

399

CHOCOLAMENT: An imbursement that is paid in chocolates. In 2001 Sainsbury's settled a lawsuit with designer Jeff Banks reputedly worth £1 million, plus a box of truffles every week for life.

400

Chocolates – emulous, amorous, fabulous.

401

Time waits for no-one but it sometimes slows down for chocolates.

402

CHOCOCLOCK: The internal clock that tells the body it is time for truffles, ganaches and pralines.

403

When time is measured in chocolates every second counts.

404

'I have seen the future and it is piped in chocolate.'
– *Epigraph to Madame de Pompadour's autobiography.*

405

The sensibilities have to be satisfied, the imagination has to be nourished, and the hopes have to be fulfilled, with chocolates.

406

CHOCOLATE FLYERS: Name given to the US pilots who parachuted bars of chocolate to the beleaguered children of Berlin during Operation Little Vittals, in the winter of 1947, and who, as a result, became the best goodwill ambassadors the US Air Force ever had.

407

CHOCOMETRICS: Using chocolates to measure or to classify. In 2003 NHS auditors in the southwest of England measured the effectiveness of care in their hospitals by keeping a record of how many boxes of chocolates – 'gestures of satisfaction' – were given to the nurses by grateful patients.

408

CHOCOPEDICS: The use of chocolates in therapy. Former chef Murray Langham developed a method for understanding behaviour and motivation based on people's chocolate preferences: people who prefer hazelnut centres, for instance, are said to be responsible, peace-loving and adaptable; and people who prefer peppermint creams are said to be changeable, extreme and versatile. People can also be a mixture of their two main preferences.

409

Chocolates are the hallmarks of taste – people are known by the chocolates they prefer.

410

It is impossible to know everything about chocolates, but not for every chocolate to know something about the impossible.

411

Chocolates – prayers worthy of frequent repetition.

412

Peaches have wept in their cream for the heavenly heart of a hazelnut praline.

413

Let us now praise individual bonbons, ballotins and bars.

414

All because the lady loves:

  Ah Cacao

  A La Reine Astrid

  Ackermans

  Alain Rolancy

  Albert Chocolatier

  Alegio Chocolaté

  Alida Marstrand

  Altmann & Kühne

  Amedei

  Amatller

  Amber Lyn

  Angelina

  Aquarelle Gourmand

  Au Chat Bleu

  Au Chocolat

  Au Parrain Généreux

Aux Délices de la Tour

Auberge du Chocolat

Auer

Bachmann

Baixas

Balducci's

Baratti & Milano

Béline

Beljoie

Bernachon

Bernard Dufoux

Bien Manger

Bissinger's

Blanxart

Bonnat

Booja Booja

Bridgewater Chocolate

Burie

Byrne & Carlson

Cacao et Chocolat

Cacao Sampaka

Café Tasse

Caffarel

Camille Bloch

Candinas Chocolatier

Carl Saint-Dié

Carrarel

Cazenave

Charbonnel et Walker

Charlemagne

Chchukululu

Chloe

Chococo

Chocolat Céleste

Chocolat Passion

Chocolate Springs

Chocolate Trading Company

Chocolaterie Bernard Callebaut

Chocolaterie Royale

Chocolaterie Wanders

Chocolats Dufoux

Chocolats Le Français

Chocolats Micheli

Chocolats Privilège

Chocolove

Christian Constant

Christian Saunal

Coco-Luxe

Cocoa Puro

Coeur Touché

Confiserie Heinemann

Coppeneur

Corné-Port Royal

Côte de France

Cuba

Cupidon

De Beussant Lachelle

De Bondt

De Granvelle

De Leaucour

De Marlieu

De Neuville

De Paula

Dagoba

Dalloyau

Damian Allsop

Daniel Giraud

Daranatz

Daskalidès

Debailleul

Debauve et Gallais

Del Rey

Deleans

Demarquette

Devries

Dolfin

Domori

Dreimeister

Droste

Druart

Duchy Originals

Dudle

Enric Rovira

Fargas

Fassbender

Fauchon

Feodora

Fiori

Fortnum & Mason

Foucher

Fouquet

Francisco Torreblanca

François Doucet

Fran's Chocolates

Frederiksberg Chokolade

Frigor

Galler

Garrison Confections

Gartner

Gérard Mulot

Gillet

Giraudi

Godiva

Gorvett & Stone

Green & Blacks

Guittard

Henriet

Hirsinger

Hotel Chocolat

Hotel Imperial

Hotel Sacher

Irsi

Jacques Bockel

Jacques Gemin

Jacques Torres

Jadis et Gourmand

Jean-Charles Rochoux

Jean-Paul Hévin

Jeff de Bruges

Joël Durand

John K. Kira's

Joseph Schmidt Confections

Joséphine Vannier

Juncal

Just William Chocolates

Kee's
Knipschildt Chocolatier
Koka
Kshocolât
L. Heiner
L. A. Burdick
L'Art de Praslin
L'Artigiano
L'Artisan du Chocolat
L'Artisan Chocolatier
L'Atelier des Douceurs
L'Atelier du Chocolat
La Bonbonnerie
La Chocolatière
La Ferme
La Fontaine au Chocolat
La Maison du Chocolat
La Mère de Famille
La Petite Marquise
La Praline Chocolatier
Läderach
Ladurée
Lalonde
Laubach
Le Chocolatier Bruyerre

Le Grand Comptoir du Chocolat

Le Nôtre

Le Palais du Chocolat

Le Roux

Legacy Chocolates

Leonidas

Les Contes de Thé

Les Palets d'Or

Letuff

Leysieffer

Li-Lac

Lindt & Sprüngli

Lulu les Chocolats

Madame de Sévigné

Maglio

Maiffret

Maison Bigot

Maison Guinget

Malagasy

Mariage Frères

MarieBelle

Marie-Claude Dutscher

Martine's

Mary

Max Brenner

Mazet de Montargis

Mélanie

Melchior Chocolates

Melt

Mendocino

Merci

Michael Recchiuti

Michel Allex

Michel Chaudun

Michel Cluizel

Micheli

Montezuma's

Moonstruck Chocolatier

Morin

Munson's

Muzzi

Neuhaus

NewTree

Nirvana

Nōka

Norman Love

Oberweis

Omanheue Cocoa Bean Company

Ortrud Münch Carstens

Over the Moon

Palais du Chocolat

Pamaco

Pancracio

Paries

Patisserie Moyne-Bressand

Patrice Chapon

Patrick Roger

Paul A. Young

Paul Wayne Gregory

Peltier

Perugina

Peter Beier Chokolade

Pierre Colas

Pierre Ginet

Pierre Hermé

Pierre Koenig

Pierre Marcolini

Pink Lady Chocolates

Poco Dolce

Poulain

Pralinette

Pralus

Prestat

Pudobeyat

Puyricard

Rabitos

Ramón Roca Chocolates

Regis

Richard Donnelly

Richart

Rococo

Romanicos

Roger's Chocolates

Roy

Santander

Sara Jayne Stanes

Saunion

Schaetjens

Scharffen Berger

Schwermer

Seven Sisters

Slitti

Soma

Special Edition Continental Chocolates

Sprüngli

Stella

Suchard

Summerbird Chocolaterie

Swan Chocolates

Sweertvaegher

Taza

TCHO

Telluride Truffle

Ten Ryen

Teuscher

The Chocolate Alchemist

The Chocolate Society

The Sinful Ballerina

Theo Confections

Thierry Mulhaupt

Thomas Haas

Torras

Truffles

Valentino

Valerie Confections

Valor

Valrhona

Van Oost

Venchi

Vermont Chocolatiers

Villars

Vivani

Vosges Haut-Chocolat

Weiss

William Curley

Wittamer

Zeller Chocolatier

Zotter

415

And especially Bendicks of Mayfair. Or, specifically, the Bendicks Bittermint. 'Dear Sir', she once wrote to the marketing manager, 'It would be enough to say that the distinctive foil wrapping, the aplanatically smooth dark couverture (95% cocoa content!), the pleasingly proportioned disc shape, and the zestful flavour of pure peppermint in a crisp, moonlight-white fondant centre, combine synergistically to fashion the most elegant and satisfying after-dinner mint there is. Yet there is more to acclaim. When holding a Bittermint, one is endowed with the kind of outer confidence and calm inner security that is proof against all distress. For the Bittermint contains within it the power to shield from any adversity, rendering us invincible in the face of endurance. Suffice to say, we should rue the days before the discovery of its curious potency. Verily, with this peerless product, let me state sincerely and without prevarication, that Bendicks have begotten not just a classic after-dinner delicacy, but the apogee of confectionery. The Bittermint is an icon of gastronomy, destined to be imitated high and low but never surpassed. Indeed, not even equalled. Long may we prosper therefore in the strength of its power, and long may we live to enjoy the refreshing taste of its superlative composition.'

And also because the lady loves her elegant chocolate *soirées* in Paris. When the final course of the candlelit dinner is finished and all the dishes have been cleared away, a butler wearing immaculate fuschia gloves places before her a sumptuous box of Debauve et Gallais chocolates. After removing the lid with care, and deftly whisking away the protective layer of tissue, the butler steps back. There is a moment of hesitation, a palpable suspense, as the lady evaluates the selection and begins to isolate her first preference. She likes to choose with care, often picking out a chocolate that matches the colour of her hair or, a favourite of hers, an attractive hand-finished ganache. She then slips it into her mouth with consummate grace and occasion. I choose more instinctively, plumping for anything that looks as if it could be a praliné. After one particularly fortuitous choice I remember nearly passing out with pleasure: a delicious symphony of subtle, nutty flavours and smooth, velvety textures, melted on my palate and released a melody of notes beyond my most elevated expectations. As the plentiful box is passed round there follows a rich and rewarding exchange of minds as each guest in turn chooses a chocolate, savours it like a fine wine, then devises an epigram of the image or allusion it evokes. Life, art and love; dreams, imagination and poetry; hopes, goals and achievements; joy, wisdom and affection – all is there in chocolates. For a chocolate is a frame of mind with some sweetness in it.

ACKNOWLEDGEMENTS

Some of the entries in *The Language of Chocolates* have appeared in the following small publications: *Sweet Inspiration* (Bruno D'Arcy, 1994); *Eating Spaghetti in the Nude* (Bruno D'Arcy, 1998); *Pic 'n' Mix* (Bruno D'Arcy, 1999); and *Thumbscrew* (Editor, Tim Kendall, 2000).

DISCLAIMER

The quotations attributed to Madame de Pompadour (as well as the ones attributed to Elizabeth Vigée-Lebrun and Prince Metternich), are as authentic as they sound, being in the spirit of what *might have been written* rather than records of what was *actually written*. In recompense for taking liberties with their names, I offer the following eulogy . . .

THE APOTHEOSIS
OF MADAME DE POMPADOUR

Clever at the clavichord
She made the highest social climb,
For first she was a courtesan
And now she is divine.
With artifice she wooed the king
At Choisy and Versailles,
And charmed the French nobility
With every flicker of her eye.

A boudoir Venus with her fan,
Her fondant looks and frothy silks,
Her heart was a cherry truffle
Under breasts as white as milk.
Flights of Boucher's rosy cherubs
Are sprinkling sugar on her brow.
Vanilla is her breath because
Her voice is even sweeter now.

Liveried footmen bearing jellies
Pay tribute to her affection –
Honour where honour is due
For a fanciful confection.
Oh! festoon her name with chocolates,
Wholly exquisite she has been,
From a royal after-dinner mint
To a beatified praline.
And 'til history dares forget the past
Her name will ever be
Enshrined in *Sèvres* porcelain,
Immortalised in *Savonnerie*.